THE DONKEY'S EASTER TALE

THE DONKEY'S EASTER TALE

Adele Colvin

Illustrated by Peyton Carmichael

PELICAN PUBLISHING COMPANY

GRETNA 2009

For Clay, Tyler, Sarah, Sam, Will, Leigh, and John
who show me the wonders of God's love everyday
—Adele Colvin

For the five parts of my heart, Ansel, Winnie, John, Will, and Andy
—Peytie Carmichael

The word "Pelican" and the depiction of a pelican
are trademarks of Pelican Publishing Company, Inc.,
and are registered in the U.S. Patent and Trademark Office.

Library of Congress Cataloging-in-Publication Data

Colvin, Adele Bibb, 1940-
  The donkey's Easter tale / by Adele Bibb Colvin; illustrated by Peyton Hamilton
Carmichael.
        p. cm.
  Summary: An old donkey tells his grandchildren about the dramatic events that
took place after he carried Jesus into Jerusalem on Palm Sunday and throughout the
week that followed.
  ISBN 978-1-58980-593-4 (hardcover : alk. paper) 1. Jesus Christ—Passion—
Juvenile fiction. 2. Jesus Christ—Resurrection—Juvenile fiction. [1. Jesus
Christ—Passion—Fiction. 2. Jesus Christ—Resurrection—Fiction. 3. Donkeys—
Fiction. 4. Holy Week—Fiction. 5. Easter—Fiction.] I. Carmichael, Peyton
Hamilton, 1940- ill. II. Title.
  PZ7.C7258Do 2009
  [E]—dc22
                                        2008030451

Printed in Singapore
Published by Pelican Publishing Company, Inc.
1000 Burmaster Street, Gretna, Louisiana 70053

THE DONKEY'S EASTER TALE

The old donkey was in his small stable. The weather was very stormy, and such times always reminded him of a Friday long ago.

In the stable with him were his two grandchildren. The little donkeys hardly ever stayed in one place long enough to talk much with their grandfather. But today, he slowly went over to them and said, "Children, while the storm is keeping us inside, I want to tell you a story, one that you have never heard."

All three lay down on some straw, and with heavy rain hammering steadily on the roof, it might have been very easy for the young ones to fall asleep. However, the minute their grandfather started speaking, they knew they would listen to his every word.

"Years ago," he began, "two strangers came to my home one Sunday morning and took me with them to a place called the Mount of Olives. There, I found myself surrounded by more strangers, and I was scared. Then several people placed their cloaks over my back and lifted a man to sit on me. I had never been ridden, so this frightened me even more, and I tried to shake him off. However, he simply leaned forward and spoke to me while gently stroking my neck. Suddenly, I was no longer afraid and was able to stand still.

"Since everyone who had gathered on the mountain that morning was going into Jerusalem to celebrate the Passover holiday, we formed a procession and started walking. Gradually, other people came to stand by the side of the road. I listened to them talking as we passed by, and, because of the things they said, I realized that the man riding on my back was *Jesus!* I was so surprised that I nearly stopped walking. The reason for my surprise was that many of my earliest memories are of stories my mother told about Jesus— first about Joseph leading my grandmother as she carried Mary to Bethlehem at the time of Jesus' birth and then how she traveled with the holy family to Egypt and back. Next, my mother told her own stories of being with Jesus while he was growing up. Years later, when I was born, a family from Bethany wanted me to live at their home, this very one.

"Now where was I? Oh, yes. As our procession continued to move, crowds lining the way grew larger and larger. Every person I saw was excited, and many of them were cheering and waving branches. I remember thinking, 'What a wonderful day this is going to be after all!'

"Before too long, we arrived in Jerusalem and went straight to the temple. Well, you are *not* going to believe what happened next! Jesus got down off my back and began turning over money tables. Then, he sent the moneychangers and tax collectors away. There were angry people everywhere I looked, and I don't mind admitting that they made me nervous.

"Jesus, however, wasn't nervous at all. He kept on until he finished clearing those men out of the temple. You should have seen the shocked expressions on some of the priests' faces when Jesus claimed they had turned his 'Father's house' into a 'den of thieves'!

"Later, as we were leaving the temple, we slowly found ourselves surrounded by people wanting to see Jesus. First, Jesus healed some who were sick, and then he began teaching. It was nearly sundown before we left for Bethany, where we were to spend the night. Personally, I was glad to be leaving Jerusalem behind because some of the men Jesus had thrown out of the temple earlier in the day may still have been angry enough to come looking for us.

"Bright and early the next morning, before we'd even had breakfast, we were out on the road once again. And just *where* do you think we went? *Back to Jerusalem and the temple!* This time the priests and officials demanded to know by what authority Jesus had come there doing and saying the things he had. I don't recall Jesus giving a specific answer to that question, but I do remember him declaring that tax collectors would be in the Kingdom of God before they, the priests, were. When he said that, those important men got even madder than they had been the day before. However, Jesus didn't seem to care and continued to teach using the stories he called 'parables' to get his point across.

"One of the parables he told that morning was about fig tree that was made to wither because it hadn't one its 'job' of producing fruit. Since the priests nd officials had not been doing their jobs proper-, I'm sure the story made them suspect that esus could be talking about them. In an effort to top him, they tried to trap him by asking all kinds f trick questions. His anger with these men rew, and he told them that the temple ould be destroyed. By chance, several riests who were leaving the temple walked y the same corner where I was waiting for esus. These men were supposed to be very owerful, but they surely looked afraid to me.

"The day had been long, and the city was hot and dusty. In the late afternoon, Jesus suggested that we all go to the Mount of Olives and rest in the shade of the trees. After we got there, I seemed to be the only one who was resting because the disciples had so many questions for Jesus. Sometimes, if I close my eyes, I think I can still hear his voice as he carefully explained to them about himself and God.

"Well, by the next day, leaders in Jerusalem were almost in a panic about the influence of Jesus' actions and teachings. During the morning, as I was again waiting for Jesus outside the temple, two men standing nearby were whispering about a deal between the chief priests and Judas Iscariot. They said Judas was going to *betray* Jesus in exchange for thirty pieces of silver. I really wished I could have told them how ridiculous that was. It had to be a mistake, just a rumor, because Judas was one of Jesus' disciples, one of his best friends. The two men soon went on their way, and with so much else going on around me, I forgot about them.

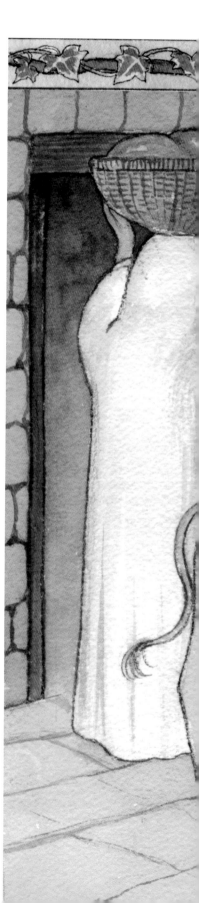

"On Thursday night of that week, Jesus and the disciples gathered to share a Passove meal in the upper room of a friend's home in Jerusalem. Jesus insisted on washing everyone' feet, and then at dinner, he made a special celebration with bread and wine. I was having m own supper outside, but through the open windows, I could hear them talking. Suddenly, stopped eating—what I had heard horrified me! Jesus said that he was about to be *betraye* by someone in that room. This could only mean that what I had heard earlier about Judas— what I had quickly dismissed as a rumor—must be *true!*

"I was trying so hard to remember the two whispering men that I nearly missed hearing another startling remark. Jesus said that before morning came, Peter, one of his closest disciples would deny *three* times that he knew Jesus. 'How can any of this be?' I wondered. 'Had Judas gone crazy? Didn't Jesus remember calling Peter the "rock" on which he would build his church?'

"None of this was making sense to me, and I was still puzzling over these questions when the meal ended and they all came outside. Judas, however, must have slipped away at some point because I didn't see him when the rest of us went with Jesus to a garden called Gethsemane.

"To be ready for whatever might happen, Jesus wanted to spend some time in prayer. He asked some of the disciples to remain there and stay awake while he prayed. But do you know what they did? They fell asleep, and I am embarrassed to say that I must have dozed off too.

"The next thing I knew there were Roman
soldiers in the garden, and they were holding swords
and spears. Worst of all, they took Jesus prisoner.
Neither of you would ever guess how the soldiers
knew which man to arrest, so I'll tell you. It seems that
Judas had arranged to lead the soldiers to the garden, and when they arrived, he walked straight to
Jesus and *kissed* him.

"Naturally everyone was terrified. We didn't
know what these men intended to do with Jesus
or what might happen to all of us. The disciples
scattered and went into hiding. Thankfully, they
thought to take me with them so I was not left
alone in the dark and at the mercy of some
Roman soldier.

"The next day was awful. First, we learned that Peter had indeed denied three different times that he'd ever known Jesus. Then, someone told us that Jesus had been taken back and forth all night long among the three most powerful men in the city for questioning.

"All week thousands of visitors had been arriving in Jerusalem for Passover. There was a custom that each year during this holiday a prisoner of the people's choice would be released. Afraid that Jesus might be the one chosen, the priests and city leaders urged everyone there to cry out against him. Pontius Pilate, the governor of Jerusalem, finally gave in to the demands of the crowd. He freed a criminal named Barabbas and ordered that Jesus be *crucified!*

"The Crucifixion was to take place just outside the city on a hill called Golgotha. Even though Jesus had been badly beaten, the soldiers forced him to walk from Pilate's fortress to that hill while carrying a heavy wooden beam. The crowd, following along, grew so large that no matter where I turned, I was unable to find a way to get to my friend. When I next saw Jesus, we were already on Golgotha.

"As the sentence was carried out, the sky turned black and a violent storm shook the earth for three hours. It was a storm like no other I have ever seen. Trees fell to the ground. Rocks broke apart. People were running in every direction, and one man kept shouting that the magnificent curtains shielding the holiest part of the temple had been torn from top to bottom. Then, in spite of all the noise and confusion, I heard Jesus speak from the cross. He said, 'Father, forgive them, for they know not what they do.'

"'How can he say such a thing,' I was wondering, 'when all the people involved in his crucifixion seemed to know exactly what they were doing?' At that instant, this thought came to me: 'God's love is for *everyone* and always will be.' Where those words came from, I did not know, but all these years, I have had the feeling that Jesus might somehow have heard my question and answered it.

"The storm ended as quickly as it had begun, and those of us near the cross knew that Jesus had died.

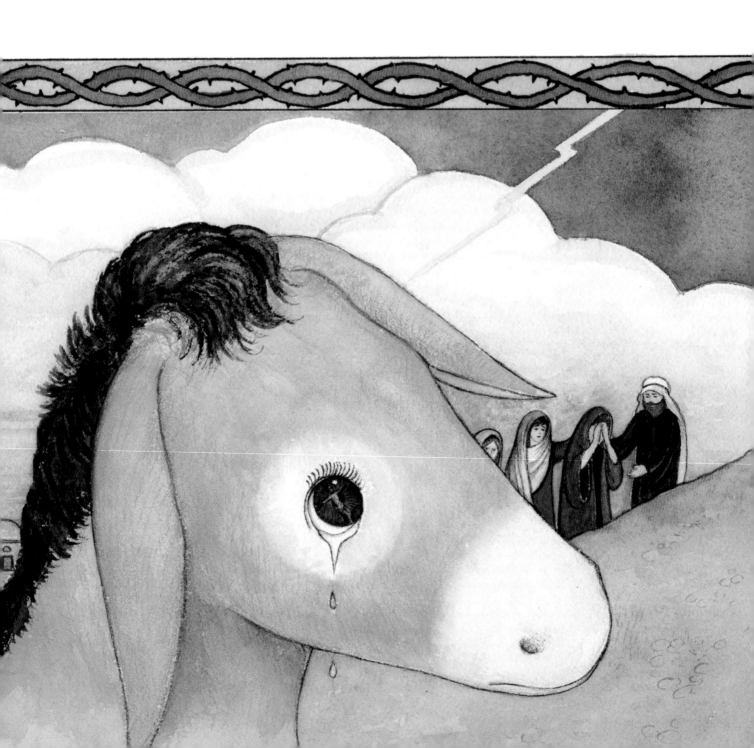

"A man named Joseph of Arimathea asked Pilate's permission to take Jesus' body to a tomb in his garden. Mary, Jesus' mother, was among those who went to this garden.

By the time we left, it was beginning to get dark; therefore, making our way along the path, I stayed close to Mary so she could put her hand on my back for balance. How I longed to be able to tell her who I was, hoping that her memories of my grandmother and mother might comfort her in some small way. During that sad walk, I could think of only her son, my holy passenger, and how much I wished that I could have done something, *anything* to protect him from the priests and soldiers.

"I don't remember much about the next day, which was Saturday, but right after dawn on Sunday, some of the women who had been loyal followers and friends of Jesus went to visit his tomb. When they got there, they couldn't believe what they saw. The huge stone that had sealed the entrance to the tomb had been rolled away. Then, an angel appeared. He said that Jesus was not there, that he was *alive*, and that he had gone to Galilee and would see them there!

"The women ran to find us, bringing this wonderful news. For a few seconds, no one spoke, and then everyone started talking at once. Suddenly, one disciple exclaimed, 'Don't you remember? He told us on Thursday night that after he was raised from the dead, he would go before us to Galilee.' Another disciple quickly recalled what Jesus had said to some priests one day. 'Destroy this temple, and in three days, I will raise it up.' Well, they had destroyed *him*, but Sunday was the *third* day, and Jesus had *risen!*

"As you can imagine, we could hardly wait to get to Galilee. When the moment finally arrived and we were once again face to face with Jesus, memories of my mother and my grandmother filled my heart. Each of us had known his gentle touch as we carried him on our backs.

"A few days later the same two men who had taken me from my home returned me to my family, right here at this very house."

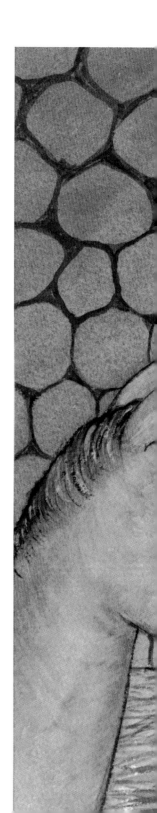

As the old donkey finished telling his story, the storm ended. Bright sunshine broke through the dark clouds and a beautiful rainbow filled the sky. The young donkeys stood up and asked excitedly, "Grandfather, can we tell your story about Jesus to our friends?" "Of course," the old donkey answered and smiled as he watched his grandchildren race to leave the stable. Just as they reached the door, he called to them, "Go and tell the story to any who will listen."

Author's Note

Could the young donkey tha
carried Jesus into Jerusalem o
Palm Sunday have remained wit
him over the next five days? If he dic
this story is the donkey's remem
brance, years later, of the dramati
events that took place throughou
that first Easter week.

The Donkey's Easter Tale i
most certainly based on Scriptura
narrative, but it is not intended as fac